BDSM CAMP

Irish Collar Series: Prequel

BRINA BRADY

DEDICATION

Thank you to all my awesome Beta Readers for helping me out until I finished my novel. Your help has been invaluable to me, and I don't know how I would have managed without your help and support. Again, thank you so much. I sincerely appreciate your help.

Ida Sue Umphers

Joy Chapman

Beta Brei-Ayn Nichole Moscato

Chapter 1

Without any clothes, Brett stepped out of the shower and into the main space of the campervan to find Sean and some young skinny guy on the bed. Brett grabbed a used towel from the floor and dried off. Sean was a Dom, but not anyone's at the moment. Brett had had no idea this trip would turn out to be a living hell. The arrangement wasn't quite what he'd had in mind. Unfortunately, he had hoped Sean would see him as a potential sub, but their agreement was for Sean to use Brett in his demonstrations at the BDSM camp in exchange for a free entrance ticket. Sean had overbooked Brett to the point he hadn't had much free time to find a Dom for himself, but somehow Sean found guys to mess around with.

"Brett, give us a few hours alone," Sean ordered using his Dom tone.

"Sure thing." Brett scanned the young guy, shooting him a death stare as he fumbled zipping up his jeans. He raced to the front of the van, grabbed Sean's cigarettes and lighter, and slipped them inside the waist of his jeans under his shirt. He let the door bang on his way outside.

The BDSM campground was outside Galway. The woodland consisted of mature trees covered in moss with a beautiful carpet of white flowers scenting the air. There was a feeling of magic. Time seemed to stop when he walked among the trees to the little stream. Sean had sold him on coming here to find a Dom. He'd also mentioned it would be an escape from the hustle and bustle of Dublin.

Brett hiked to the area where a thick log had fallen near the stream and sat. The BDSM demonstrations began after dinner and tomorrow night they had a meet-and-greet for unattached Doms and subs. Right now though, he had a few hours to disappear. He pulled out a cigarette and lit it. Sean had paid for the campervan and his ticket here, so he couldn't say anything to him. He hadn't been stuck like this since he was a child, and he had no intention of giving up his freedom when he returned to Dublin. He was always worried how he looked since he was a boy. Sean made him feel ugly. Brett pulled out a mirror and put his green bandanna around his forehead through his brown hair. His eyes looked bluer than gray today from the color of his shirt. Sean didn't much notice his eyes changed colors from what he was wearing.

An older man stopped in front of him. He wore a tight navy T-shirt and tight jeans. His chest was impressively muscled.

Please be available. Like me. Collar me.

"I'm Master Cleary." His blue eyes twinkled as he said his name.

Brett inhaled, then exhaled his smoke away from Master Cleary. "Brett Dalton, sir."

"You sound like you're from England." Master Cleary sat beside him.

"I was born there but moved here."

"Why are you here alone?"

"I came here with a Dom, and he's with some twink in the campervan. I had to disappear for a couple of hours."

Master Cleary frowned. "Is he your Dom?"

"No, sir. He paid for my ticket in exchange for using me as his model during his demonstrations. That was the deal."

"You look upset."

"I have nowhere to go while he's with the twink. This is the third day in a row I've had to get lost."

"What about dinner?"

"I don't know, sir. I have a feeling he's going to use my dinner ticket on the new twink."

"I have an extra dinner ticket and you can meet my two subs."

"Thank you, sir." No one had ever cared if he missed a meal or not. This stranger was already one of the kindest men he had met. Right off, Master Cleary helped him when he was doomed to be alone and hungry.

"Come with me to my campervan. You can hang out with us until you're needed for the demonstrations."

Master Cleary was the perfect Dom he had read about in gay BDSM romance books, good-looking and kind to others. How did he manage two subs? His van was brand new indicating he was a provider and accomplished. He followed Master Cleary inside.

"Brett, this is Jack and Kevin. Boys, this is Brett. He's been displaced for a few hours."

Brett noted how Jack's cornflower blue eyes contrasted with his ruddy complexion. His nose was sprinkled with freckles, cute. Kevin was slightly taller, with the same brown hair as Jack's and darker blue eyes.

"And I'm Aiden." Another young man spoke as he came out of the restroom. Brett envied Aiden's collar-length blond hair. He looked to be around the same age as he was.

"I didn't know you were here," Master Cleary said. "All of you stay here, I have to talk to Dr. Murray privately." Master Cleary kissed Kevin and Jack before he left the van.

"What happened?" Jack asked.

"The Dom I came down here with is with some twink. He told me to leave for a couple of hours. Master Cleary brought me here. If you guys want me gone, I'll leave."

"No way. You sound like you've been through enough shit," Kevin said.

"So, does your Dom cheat on you all the time?" Jack asked.

"That's the thing. He's not my Dom. We work together at Murphy's Pub in Dublin. He asked me to be his model for his demonstrations."

"But do you want him to be your Dom?" Jack asked.

"I did before we got here. I can see now he doesn't see me that way."

"Damn. You need to find your own Dom. There are lots of them here looking for subs."

"I'm going to look at the meet-and-greet." As it was for unattached subs and Doms, Sean told him he should find a Dom and he'd look for a sub.

"Do you have chaps and leather clothing?"

"At the campervan." Brett hadn't thought about his clothes for tonight being at the van. He didn't much care about walking in on Sean and the twink.

"You look around my size. You can borrow some of mine if he won't let you back in," Kevin offered.

"Thanks."

Brett changed into the chaps and leather vest. Kevin was right, they wore the same size.

Master Cleary returned.

"Let's go to dinner. Dr. Murray saved an extra seat so Brett can join us."

"Thank you, Master Cleary." Brett smiled to cover his anxiety when anyone showed him kindness. For some strange reason it made him teary-eyed and had him feeling like he belonged here with them. Most men barked orders or insulted him in some way. Master Cleary was the kind of Dom he wished he could find for himself.

Once they were outside, they hiked along the path to the Mess Hall for dinner. All sorts of men filled up most of the tables. Some dressed in leather while others dressed casually in jeans. Brett scanned the room for Sean, but he didn't see him anywhere. Maybe he could spend the rest of the evening with Master Cleary and his boys.

Brett sat between Jack and Aiden. Jack and Kevin wore mini-Master Cleary leather outfits. Brett wished he had a Dom who would dress him like his mini version. Master Cleary and Dr. Murray sat across from them at the table. Dr. Murray looked like a rockstar instead of a doctor. He had the same gray eyes as Brett, but his sparkled with mischief. Dr. Murray's light hair had golden highlights under the lights.

Brett noticed he was the only one without a collar. He often made-up stories about his present circumstances, so, in his mind, he was like others, and pretended he belonged to Master Cleary.

"We're going to sign up for some of the activities. Which ones are you signed up for?" Kevin asked.

"Sean didn't mention I had to sign up for them." He hated the way Sean treated him. He didn't want him for a sub, but he behaved like he didn't want Brett to find his own Dom. None of it made sense. He only used Brett for demonstrations.

"You can just go where we go. There are last minute sign-ups," Jack said.

As Brett cut his steak, Sean and the skinny guy walked past their table without stopping, but Sean's eyes caught his before they picked up the pace.

"What's the name of the Dom you're here with?" Dr. Murray asked.

"Sean Casey, sir."

"Is he from Dublin?"

"Yes, we both are." Brett didn't like the doctor's questions and the lovely welcome feeling dispersed with them.

"Be very careful who you play with here and always use protection," Dr. Murray said.

"So far, I haven't played with anyone."

While Brett enjoyed his chocolate ice cream topped with whipped cream and a cherry, someone tapped him on the shoulder. He turned around to see who it was.

Chapter 2

Sean was dressed in his black leather, which caused Brett's cock to twitch. He was about a head taller than Brett, had the most beautiful blond hair, and his face was stunning. Sean was irresistible to every damn sub in Dublin, from his cleft chin to his sparkling blue eyes. The expression on Sean's face indicated he was displeased with Brett for enjoying himself without him. That look meant Sean was about to do something to kill Brett's joy.

"I need you, boy. Now." Sean pulled Brett's chair back.

Master Cleary said, "It's very rude for you to demand Brett leave with you. He's still eating. You can wait."

"Brett is with me, and he's none of your damn business."

"You're not his Dom and you'd do well if you remembered that," Master Cleary said.

"Thank you for the dinner ticket," Brett told Master Cleary and quickly got up and followed Sean to his booth. He wanted to finish his dessert but once again Sean had messed with his chance to meet people and enjoy something as simple as ice cream.

"I see you found some friends," Sean said.

"I did."

"Remember to keep yourself free for me and the demonstrations."

"You didn't seem to care where I went before when you were fucking that skinny guy."

"Don't judge my behavior."

"I'm stating the facts, not judging anything. Thanks to Master Cleary who took pity on me and let me hang out with them when you were fucking around, I at least got dinner."

"That Cleary guy is a little too interested in you."

"He has two subs and one more wouldn't change much."

"Dream on, Brett. Pay attention. It's time for us to do the demonstration."

"Yes, sir." Brett had promised to be his model, and he'd follow through on his side of the agreement.

"Tonight, I'm demonstrating the use of the St. Andrew's Cross. It's a freestanding one. I'm going to use leather restraints and various spanking implements. Are you okay with that?"

"Yes, sir." All Brett wanted to do was please Sean, so he'd choose him to be his sub, but after three days with Sean hooking up with three different guys, he no longer stood a chance. At this point he wasn't sure he even wanted Sean anymore. Every time he was in his presence, he wanted to bury himself in a hole. Why did Sean make him feel like an immature brat? Sean had told him several times he needed to return to school because he wasn't intelligent enough to be his sub or anyone else's. Sean even called Brett stupid in front of others, especially at work.

"Where did you get those clothes?"

"One of the guys lent them to me because you were busy, and I couldn't get mine."

"I brought your clothes in a bag. Wear your own clothes. Return those tonight." Sean used his angry Dom voice.

"Yes, sir." Brett took the bag from the table and went to the restroom to change. He dressed in a stall and came out wearing his leather shorts, a leather vest, and his black boots. A huge leather man whistled at him. Brett's face warmed into a blush. He wanted attention but as soon as he received some, he wanted to hide.

"I see you're not collared. Does that mean you don't have a Dom?"

"Yes, sir."

"Why don't you do a scene with me later?"

"When and where, sir?" The huge man resembled a bald pirate wearing leather.

"At eleven in my campervan." He pulled out his phone and handed it to Brett. "Add your number. What's your name?"

"Brett Dalton from Dublin, sir." Brett added his name and number and returned the phone.

"I'm Master Colin. My van is in spot 203. Be there at eleven."

"Yes, sir."

Brett bumped into Aiden and Dr. Murray in the men's room.

"Be careful," Dr. Murray warned.

"I will, sir." Brett figured Dr. Murray had heard his exchange with Master Colin. Brett rushed back to Sean's booth in the main room before he started yelling at him in public.

"What took you so long?"

"Some Dom asked me to play with him tonight."

"Where and who?" Sean shouted.

"Look, I agreed to be your model. Once the job is over, I'm on my own."

"Don't talk to me like that! You're going to regret disrespecting me."

"You don't want me, but you act like you don't want me finding a Dom. That's not fair."

"Shut up! People are waiting for the demonstration. Follow my directions."

"Yes, sir." Brett was so annoyed with Sean holding him back. He was the same way at work. He made sure no one flirted with him and had cock blocked him so many damn times.

Brett checked out all the Doms and subs sitting on folding chairs. There were so many of them.

"I'm going to introduce you to the St. Andrew's Cross in this session." Sean pointed to the cross. "If you want to build one, make it out of strong material. It must hold the weight of a man. I'll be using Brett as my model tonight." Sean pointed at Brett. "We've done many scenes together. Are you ready, Brett?"

"Yes, sir."

"The first thing you must decide as a Dom is do you want your sub to face the cross or face you. Brett is going to face the cross because I'm going to use some spanking implements on his ass." Sean pointed to the cross and Brett faced it.

"If Brett were my sub, I'd make him remove his clothes. That's also a personal choice. Before you play, ask your partner or sub their safeword like this." Sean walked in front of Brett. "What's your safeword and what does it mean?"

"Red is to stop, yellow is to pause for communication, and green is keep going, I'm fine."

"Spread your arms and feet wide so I can cuff you."

Brett's nerve endings tingled with eagerness. For a moment, he didn't understand why Sean acted like he cared for him, but then he realized he was in front of his peers being judged. Brett thought he had no reason to be concerned even though he had made the threat he would pay for being disrespectful to him.

"I'm going to fasten you up. If it's too tight, let me know. Are you ready?"

"Yes, sir."

Sean fastened his wrists first, leaving him standing on his toes. He clicked the leather cuffs to his ankles on both sides of the cross, then wrapped a few belts around his body to take the pressure off Brett's wrists and ankles. Brett tested to see if he could move, but he couldn't. His ass cheeks clenched at what was to come; the anticipation was killing him.

"What color are you?" Sean asked.

"Green, sir."

"Any questions up to this point?" Sean asked the audience. "Yes." Sean pointed to someone's raised hand.

"Did you discuss which spanking implements you plan to use before you hooked him up?" Master Cleary asked.

Brett was relieved to hear Master Cleary was in the audience. So, whatever Sean had in mind, he might curb it knowing there was someone on his side. Brett loved Master Cleary.

"No. As I said before if you were listening, Brett has been my model many times and done scenes with me. I know his soft and hard limits."

"If you didn't know him, would you discuss his limits?"

"Yes, but I know Brett, so it's not a problem."

"Thank you, Sean," Master Cleary said.

Brett wondered if Dr. Murray was with Master Cleary. He couldn't see since he was facing the cross. Sean would have a shit fit if he turned his head.

"Before you use any implement, make sure your boy is warmed up. Some Doms like to spank their sub over their lap. I'm going to use a flogger since it's a soft swat. There are many different floggers." Sean picked one up. "This one is made of leather with eighteen strands. Each leather fall has been cut at an angle for a tip with a bite. You can use this flogger for a good stinging. You can purchase one like this at the gift shop. It's called the Strict Leather Flogger and sells at a reasonable price. Any questions?"

"Yes. Do you think a flogger with angled tips is the best implement to warm up a sub's ass?" Dr. Murray asked.

"Of course, a bare ass over the knee spanking with your hand would be the best, but Brett doesn't want to be naked in public. I respect his request. He enjoys this particular flogger."

"Thank you, Sean."

"I'm going to swat him five times, then I'll switch to another implement."

Sean landed the first swat on his ass, stinging. Brett knew he was angry at him and now with Master Cleary and Dr. Murray asking him questions to make him look bad, Sean would take out his anger on Brett like he always did.

After the second swat, Brett felt the tips digging at his ass. He was going to stop thinking and experience the pain, hoping it would take him to subspace. The good thing about Sean, he took Brett to subspace fast. It happened a lot faster when he was naked, but he loved the sound of leather hitting leather. Sean had used leather polish, so it smelled brand new. He inhaled the scent as he accepted each swat.

"Hey, Brett, what color are you?" Sean asked.

"Green, sir."

"The next implement I'll use is a paddle with holes." Sean held it up for everyone to see.

The first swat landed hard and grabbed his absolute attention instantly. Brett's cock twitched as his ass jiggled from the heavy-handed impact.

Sean traced his hand on the small of Brett's back. "Stay still." He kissed Brett's ear. "Don't ever disrespect me." Sean's minty breath traveled to his nose.

"I'm sorry, sir." Brett squeezed his eyes closed.

"Act like it then," Sean ordered.

Brett didn't budge while Sean struck his ass again, and his cock hardened.

"Ass out," Sean ordered.

Brett stuck out his ass as ordered. Sean made sure he didn't have any pleasure, only pain.

Sean issued a series of stinging blows from the wooden paddle. The meaner Sean had gotten, the more Brett's cock stiffened against his stomach. He needed the pain, the release from messing up and displeasing Sean. He needed that mean Sean in his life because he took him to subspace, but it sure would be nice to have Master Cleary, or someone like him, take him to subspace.

"Brett, are you here with me?"

"Yes, sir."

"Good boy." Sean ran his fingers through Brett's hair. The slight caress of Sean's fingertips helped Brett relax. Soothing, caring, and so unlike Sean, yet Brett relished the rare moments when he demonstrated he cared on some level.

He stopped thinking and focused on the sensation of Sean's fingers touching his hair, face, and scalp.

"If at any time you feel your sub or partner is losing his surroundings, talk to him to make sure he's okay. Brett tends to disappear when he's climbing into subspace. Slow down what you're doing if you sense them hitting subspace before you want them there. Any questions?"

"Do you ever stop your sub from going to subspace?" asked a voice Brett didn't recognize.

"If we're working on edging, then I'd try to stop him from moving into it. But edging can be dangerous. Don't let it go on too long and make sure he has some release, whether it's subspace or the other. I have one more implement I want to use. Are you okay, Brett?"

"Yes, sir."

Sean picked up a whip. "If your partner enjoys being spanked and you're ready to add a whip to your play, selecting the right one to fit your desires can be more complicated than you think. What I'm doing is called impact play. That includes spanking, whipping, flogging, and caning. The whip should only hit body parts protected by fat or muscle. I only whip the butt or thighs."

Sean had whipped him three times when Brett shouted, "Red."

Sean stopped swinging and quickly went up to Brett. "What's wrong?"

"Red, sir."

"Okay. I'm going to take you down."

He released Brett from his belts and cuffs and handed him a bottle of water.

"Sometimes, they use their safeword. You don't want to work with anyone who doesn't use their safeword. Brett knows when to stop. Want to lie down?"

"No, sir," Brett growled at Sean. "Am I done for the night?"

"Yes. I'll see you at the van in fifteen minutes. We need to talk."

"Yes, sir." Brett slipped out of Sean's booth and left the building heading to the wooded path on the way to the campervan. He was ready to explode. Sean knew he didn't ever want to be whipped. He had it written in his files that Sean stored on his laptop. He'd literally ignored his hard boundary. What Dom does shit like that?

He pulled out a cigarette, lit it, and continued walking. He needed to forget what happened and rest up for later. At eleven he had to meet Master Colin.

Hopefully, he'd let him stay overnight and he could have some time away from Sean.

As soon as he reached the van, he stood around and waited for Sean, who had never given him his own key. Brett paced back and forth until Sean finally arrived. He was alone this time.

He unlocked the door, and Brett followed him inside.

"What the hell happened?" Sean asked.

"Did you forget whipping is a hard limit for me? Or do you have so many guys you forgot?"

"I told you I'd get back at you for disrespecting me. I could have hurt you more."

"You're not a real Dom. I should have told everyone you broke the rules."

"Don't you ever threaten me, boy. I'll make you suffer, but not in front of your new friends. Then again, I could tell our boss you stole the money and covered it up."

"That's a damn lie. You know it wasn't me."

"Do you think Andy will believe you or me?"

"I'm going back out to look at the demonstrations." Brett walked toward the door.

"Be back here by one. If not, you don't sleep here," Sean shouted.

Chapter 3

Brett had a few hours before he had to meet Master Colin. On his way to the Mess Hall, he sat down on an empty bench to smoke another cigarette before he went inside to check out all the demonstrations and maybe catch up with Master Cleary and the boys. He was miserably sore from Sean's damn whip. Whatever possessed Sean to use a whip? By the angry expression painted on his face in the campervan, he wasn't done making him suffer for being disrespectful to him.

When Brett finished smoking, he hurried along the path to enter the main building where the demonstrations were. He showed the man at the door his ID card then walked to the back area where double doors were opened to the Mess Hall, but it was empty. He saw a food stand at the beginning of the hallway and ordered a fizzy drink. He returned to the demonstration area and stopped by a booth with rope displays. The rope Dom was setting up the area. He used helpers to tie three men to chairs. Brett was really interested in this Japanese man and his rope.

"Hey, Brett!"

Brett turned around and Master Cleary stood with Jack and Kevin at his side.

"Are you guys signed up?" Brett asked.

"Yes, we're up in thirty minutes, but we wanted to watch first," Kevin said.

"I want to watch too." Brett pushed his hair out of his eyes.

"Jack and Kevin, sit over there and wait for your turn. I need to talk to Brett." Master Cleary pointed to two empty folding chairs.

"You want to talk to me, sir?" Brett didn't know if this was a good or bad thing.

"Privately. Follow me."

Brett trailed Master Cleary outside and worried what he wanted to talk to him about. His mind refused to shut off. All the what-ifs invaded his thoughts in a vicious circle. A heaviness came over him as he took in a large breath. He constantly told himself he was overreacting to damn near everything. Calm down.

"Tell me about the whip," Master Cleary said.

"What do you mean, sir?" Brett knew exactly what he meant, but he was afraid Master Cleary would look down on him for being such a pussy for using his safeword.

"Is whipping a soft or hard limit for you?"

"Please don't tell anyone if I tell you." Brett refused to lie to Master Cleary since he probably could detect a lie immediately.

"Whatever you say to me is between us." Master Cleary furrowed his brows.

"I hate whips and Sean knows that. He did it on purpose because he said I disrespected him. I did the only thing I could think of which was to use my safeword." As soon as Brett told the truth to Master Cleary his burden of fear lessened. He believed the secrets he kept could be turned over to Master Cleary as there was no doubt he'd help him when he was in need. He had that one person who would be there for him. Something he hadn't had since Mr. Bailey and even he had turned on Brett in the end.

"Be very careful with him." Master Cleary handed him his business card. "My phone number is on this card. Give me your phone and I'll program it in there as well in case you lose my card."

Brett handed him his phone. He had worried over nothing again. Master Cleary was here supporting him, not Sean. Master Cleary made him feel worthy of happiness, which Sean didn't provide on any level. He scanned the card. Master Cleary owned a pub in Galway.

"I've known Sean for three years. He has helped me more than he has hurt me. He usually gets over being mean." Brett didn't want Master Cleary to think Sean was all bad.

"Hard limits are established and negotiated at the top and are never to be crossed during scene play. If I see him breaking rules, I'll make sure he is banned from the BDSM camp."

"He doesn't break rules when he's playing with a sub, just with me."

"You told me he doesn't want you to be his sub. Why do you waste your time with him?" Master Cleary rested his eyes on Brett, patiently waiting for him to respond.

"Even though he gets mean, he saved me from a bad situation. He also helped me get a job in Dublin."

"Do you have parents?"

"I ran away from them. They locked me up in a basement and sometimes starved me. I was never allowed to have friends. One day, something very bad happened. Instead of going home, I ran away to Ireland."

"Where are they now?"

"Scotland. They don't know where I am."

"What caused you to leave?"

"My younger sister disappeared and I think they did something to her."

"I'm sorry you had a horrible upbringing. I wish I could take away all your pain, but I can help you when you need it from now on."

"Thanks."

"Please don't smoke. It's bad for your health. I would hate to see you in trouble or get sick."

"I'll try to stop. These aren't my cigarettes. They belong to Sean. I took them because he kicked me out of the van. He didn't even notice."

"That's stealing. You need to return them."

"I will, sir."

"Remember, if you find yourself in trouble, call me. You're not alone."

"Thank you, sir."

Later Sean stopped him by stepping in front of him. "Hey, give me my cigarettes!" Sean shouted at him.

Brett shifted his weight from side to side. His face heated bright red. He handed him the pack of cigarettes.

"Don't steal my cigarettes again or there will be a high price to pay. Where's my lighter?" Sean stretched his arm out with his palm up.

Brett dug it out of the front pocket of his short leather pants.

Later that evening, Brett said good night to the group and left for the path to Master Colin's campervan. He was excited to do a scene with him and maybe more would come of it. He knocked on the door. Master Colin opened it. He was dressed in jeans and a gray T-shirt. But why would he ask him to play with him in his van instead of the private rooms at the main building?

"Sit down, boy."

Brett sat down on the folding chair in the kitchen. The van was not new like Master Cleary's, but extremely old with a musty smell. He didn't know anything about Master Colin, but he needed a Dom and since he'd asked him here, the man must like something about him. At least, he hoped so.

"What are your hard limits?" Master Colin asked.

"Whips, water sports, humiliation, and breath play."

"What is your safeword?"

"Red, sir."

"Where do you live?"

"Dublin, sir."

"Strip off your clothes. I want to see you, all of you."

Brett looked around the van to see if there were any spanking implements, ropes, or cuffs. He didn't see anything resembling BDSM toys, and he didn't smell any leather. Was this man a Dom or an imposter? He didn't make him feel like Master Cleary had. Brett's safety veil disappeared the minute he had stepped inside. Master Colin's campervan was parked so far from Sean's and Master Cleary's. What had he gotten himself into? He should have told someone what spot number Master Colin parked in.

"Strip, boy! I don't like to repeat myself."

Something was off in this van. This wasn't what Brett wanted. His entire reason for being here was to find a Dom.

"What's the problem, boy?"

What had made him think this was a good idea? Before he could answer, Master Colin grabbed him and cuffed his hands behind his back. He threw him on the thin makeshift couch. The van reeked of whiskey and tobacco. Ashtrays were filled with old cigarette butts.

"I don't feel safe, sir."

"You agreed to meet me here for a scene. That's what we're going to do."

"I don't know, sir. I want to leave."

"Get out!" Master Colin's face turned apple red.

"I need my cuffs removed first, sir."

Master Colin pulled him from the couch, dragged him across the room, and opened the door. He shoved Brett outside where he landed on his ass. When he looked up to see where Master Colin was, the door slammed. He had no idea how he was going to remove the cuffs. His first thoughts were to run before he changed his mind and forced him to do a scene with him or hurt him in some way.

He picked himself up and started walking in the dark. He had made a fool of himself by his own choices. An hour later, he found Sean's campervan. Since he didn't have a key and his hands were cuffed, he used his boot to kick the door. He kicked several times, but no one answered. There was no way to know if Sean was in there or not.

He turned around and walked back to Master Cleary's. Brett hated to bother him at this late hour, but he'd said to call him if he was in trouble. He couldn't call him with handcuffs on. Once he saw the lights were on, he figured they were up, but he didn't feel right interrupting them. He found a spot to lie down for the night. Luckily it was summer, he thought, as tears rolled down his cheeks and he couldn't wipe them away.

Chapter 4

The campervan door squeaked open. "Brett, what happened?" Master Cleary asked.

"How did you know I was out here?" Brett thought he had been quiet.

"I heard some noise. Tell me what happened."

"I ran into some trouble," Brett said.

"Did Sean handcuff you?" Master Cleary demanded in full-blown Dom mode.

"No, sir. Master Colin did. I met him at his van. He cuffed me and threw me out when I asked to leave."

"There is no Master Colin registered at the camp. I'm going to unlock them with my universal handcuff key. I'll help you up." Master Cleary picked him up and he followed him inside the van.

Jack and Kevin sat together on the bed and were writing in their notebooks. He envied their intimacy with each other and love for Master Cleary. They had what he had desired all his life.

"Brett ran into some trouble. I need to remove the cuffs."

"Who did that?" Jack asked.

"This Dom I was going to have a scene with, but I freaked out, and wanted to leave. He handcuffed me and threw me out. Literally. I went to Sean's campervan, but he never answered the door."

Master Cleary removed his keychain from his belt loop and used the master key to free Brett from his cuffs. "Sit with the boys and relax. I'm going to follow up on Master Colin. I want to know who he is and where he came from." He set the cuffs on the counter, then gave Brett a bottle of water. "Drink this."

"Thank you, sir." Brett wanted to belong to Master Cleary, but he knew there was no way he could share a Dom, much as he liked Jack and Kevin.

"I packed sleeping bags so you can sleep on the floor. I don't want you roaming around outside. Colin could be looking for you."

"I don't want to ruin your evening."

"Go on." Master Cleary pulled the sleeping bag out from a tiny closet and handed it to Brett.

"It's all my fault for trusting him, sir."

"Don't go to anyone's campervan. Do scenes inside the private rooms where all the Doms have been approved."

"Yes, sir."

Master Cleary scrolled through his phone and said, "Master Colin has not been approved to do scenes in private rooms. He's not a paid member of the BDSM camp. He's an imposter. Where is his campervan parked?"

"Spot 203." Brett put his head down on the sleeping bag.

"Are you okay?" Jack asked.

"I freaked out when I thought I wouldn't ever get the cuffs off, but I'm okay now. It just makes me think how stupid and trusting I am."

Master Cleary walked to the front and opened the door. "I'm going outside to make a phone call."

"Would you consider being Master Cleary's sub with us?" Jack asked.

"Jack! Master Cleary makes those types of decisions," Kevin shouted.

"I like Master Cleary and would love if he were my Dom, but I can't share a Dom. Sorry, but I need my own. I'd go crazy. I like hanging out with you guys, though." Brett wished he lived closer to them because they always accepted him and were willing to help through some bad times at the camp.

"He is a great Dom. He really wasn't looking for two subs, but he fell in love with us. He said he knew we wouldn't be happy if we were separated. He's been so good sharing his time with each of us separately and all together," Jack said.

"Do you three have sex all together."

"Yes, we do and also separately," Kevin said.

"What is it like?"

"It can get crazy sometimes, but we do a lot of laughing," Kevin said.

"Master Cleary decides where his dick goes. We never know but eventually he'll get to both of us," Jack said.

"I'm glad you two have a good Dom."

"We came from a bad Dom, and he made us do bad things. We ran away when he told us to kill someone," Kevin said.

"Kill someone? That's serious. I'm glad you're safe now," Brett said.

"He was mean to us," Jack said.

"I hope I don't end up with a mean one." Brett pushed his hair out of his eyes.

"If he is, leave like we did." Kevin nodded with Jack.

Master Cleary returned to the van. "What were you guys talking about?"

"I asked Brett if he wanted you to be his Dom," Jack admitted.

"I would love Brett to be my sub, but I have two subs which are more than enough. Brett will find his own Dom."

"I sure hope so, sir." Hearing Master Cleary state he would love to have him as a sub meant a great deal, especially when he'd failed in his mission to find a Dom.

"You will. Please don't take chances on Doms you don't know a thing about. Colin was escorted out of the campgrounds, so he won't be back to bother you."

"Thanks, sir."

In the morning, they took showers at the bathing area. After breakfast, they met back in the main hall where the demonstrations were.

Sean prowled forward to Brett. "Where the hell were you all night?"

"I had to stay with Master Cleary since you didn't answer the door."

"Don't do shit like that again. You have a phone. Why didn't you call me?"

"I couldn't. I had some issues."

"We have to talk about something."

Brett turned away from Sean to ignore him, but he grabbed Brett's shoulder and spun him around.

"Now!" Sean crossed his arms, broadening his stance and displaying his bulged muscles to further intimidate Brett.

"What's so important?"

"Follow me outside. It's not for everyone to hear."

Brett trailed behind Sean. He had no idea what was so important. Most likely he planned to kick him out of the campervan. It wouldn't surprise him if he did. Sean could be his best friend one minute then shortly turn into his worst enemy. He had weighed the possibility of Sean leaving him to fend for himself before he had accepted his invitation to help during the demos. He thought it was worth the chance because he truly believed he would find a Dom who would love him.

Once they reached an area with no one around, Sean grabbed his shoulders again. "Listen to me. I'm not your Dom, but I'm responsible for you. I worried where you were last night. Tell me what happened."

"Some Dom handcuffed me then threw me out of his campervan."

"Who?"

Brett saw the same expression on Sean when he cock blocked him at Murphy's Pub. "Master Colin."

"He threw you out with handcuffs on you?"

"Yes. Master Cleary helped me get them off."

"Remember I told you I might find a way for you to make money?"

Brett nodded.

"If you take part in a special scene with me, we can earn five hundred euros. The camp hasn't approved it. It's a competition between a group of Doms. This rich man will pay the winner the money."

"To do what?"

"I thought you'd be jumping for it."

"I want the money, but what kind of scene, sir?"

"Do you trust me?"

"Sometimes. Why won't you tell me what I have to do for that money?"

"I will tie you in a wire cage hanging parallel to the ground between two trees. You have to be naked. There will be an electric spinner like in a rotisserie...like I'm roasting you over a small fire."

"You want to roast me naked in a wire cage over fire?" Brett couldn't believe his ears. He had to be joking.

"Think about the money. It's going to be you and two other subs with their Doms doing the scene. It will be a competition to see which sub can last the longest without using their safeword."

"What if I burn?"

"You won't burn. I'll make sure you won't. You can use your safeword to stop at any point, but we won't get the money. I really want you to do this with me."

Sean switched to his kind friend voice. "Let me figure something out about the money. How about if I give you a hundred euros for trying even if you want to safeword out. Would you consider it?"

"Where is the money coming from?"

"It's coming from a rich old man."

This was what made him still stay with Sean, even though he had two sides. Any time his friendly side came out, he wanted something from Brett. He liked to try new things and he needed the money, but anything with fire wasn't something he felt safe with. Was the money worth it? If he had enough money, he could save it for bad times.

"I don't know. I need the money, but that doesn't sound like something I want to do."

"If you win, we could do this demonstration all around the BDSM clubs and get money for it. It can open up a new world for us."

"Sean, we're not an 'us.' You told me you're not interested in me. Now you want me to be part of your unapproved demo. I need to think about it more."

"You mean you want to ask Master Cleary if you should do it. I told you this is a secret and doesn't have anything to do with the camp. Do not tell him anything about it. I'll know if you do."

"How do I know I won't get burned from the fire?"

"The cage will be much higher than the little fire underneath you."

"What if it doesn't hold me up and I drop into the fire?"

"We can practice and make sure it can hold you without a fire under you. Give it a try. What do you have to lose?"

"My fucking skin. I don't want to be roasted like a pig."

"You either trust me or you don't. Who saved you from your last job?"

"You did."

"Did I have to save you?"

"No. I'm happy you helped me out of a bad situation."

"Let me spice this deal for you. If you do this with me, I'll collar you. You want a Dom and I need a sub. What do you think of that?"

"So, all of a sudden you want to collar me if I help you?"

"Hey, why do you think I asked you to come with me?"

"To be your demo model. If you were so into me, why haven't you fucked me yet?" Brett didn't wait for an answer. He ran from Sean back inside the building.

Chapter 5

Brett found Jack and Kevin in the gift shop. They were buying Master Cleary a black shirt with Dom written in gold across the chest. He caught Jack's eye when he stopped near him.

"Hey, what do you think?" Jack held up the shirt for Brett to see.

"It's perfect for Master Cleary." Brett wished he had a Dom to buy a shirt for. The isolation from others deepened when he was the only guy without a Dom. He suffered and no one understood or cared even if there were other guys doomed to suffer his fate. Recently things had changed, or so it seemed. He could seek comfort from others or withdraw to compose himself alone. He would check if Jack and Kevin cared for him as a friend or if it was all for show. Many times, his friendships were only one way. Once a friend didn't need Brett, they left him and moved on with other friends. After Brett served a purpose, they would leave him.

"Is something wrong?" Kevin asked

"Can I run something by you two?"

"As soon as we're done here." Kevin paid for the shirt and three soft drinks. The clerk placed the shirt into a bag for them. Jack passed out the drinks as they followed Brett out of the store to the display area.

"Thanks." Brett thought the drink was for Master Cleary. It surprised him they had bought him one too. They always made him feel part of the group. "Let's go outside," he suggested.

They left the building and sat on the front steps with Brett sitting between them. All three grabbed their sunglasses and put them on. Brett loved the sun, but it was brighter than he thought it would be. He watched as men dressed in leather walked into the building. Some had subs while others entered alone. Why couldn't one of those unattached Doms pick him?

Brett's father told him he was ugly and not to expect anything to be easy. Those words were imprinted on his mind. The old man could say the vilest things to him when he was growing up. The woman they lived with was not his birth mother, and she was as vile as his father. Brett had no idea what had happened to his real mother, but he had imagined his father disposed of her one way or another.

"So what do you want to run by us?"

"Sean wants me to do a special demo competition with him. If I win, he will collar me."

"So, if you do good, he'll collar you? That doesn't sound like he cares about you," Kevin said.

"I need a Dom. I have to start somewhere. No one wants me because I don't have any collared sub experience."

"It's not like getting job experience. Your Dom should love you no matter what," Jack said.

"You guys don't get it. I'm not loveable. I never was and never will be."

"What do you mean?" Jack asked.

"I had cruel parents. They hated me. That's why I ran away."

"Did they hate you because you were gay?" Kevin asked.

"No. They didn't know I was gay. They kept me in the basement and sometimes they starved me."

"Did you go to school?"

Brett nodded. He wondered if they thought he was stupid.

"Why didn't you tell your teacher?" Kevin asked.

"I was too afraid to say anything. I wasn't allowed any friends. You two and Aiden are the closest I've gotten to having real friends in a long time."

"Sorry your childhood sounds like mine, "Jack said.

"We're both your friend and Aiden said he liked hanging out with you. Master Cleary will always help you. He doesn't like to see or hear about any sub being abused. He gets right on it," Kevin said.

"You two were lucky to find him."

"You'll get one. Keep looking," Jack said.

"What do you have to do with Sean?" Kevin asked again.

"Go in a turning cage over fire."

"No. No. You'll get burned alive. Don't do it," Kevin said.

"Sean might be a walking sex machine, but he's a big con. It sounds like he'll make money if he can roast you alive. Don't do it," Jack said.

"Okay. Then I'll tell him no." Brett knew there had to be some risk for him to get paid, but he wanted a Dom more than he wanted the money. He could not tell either of them he planned to do it.

"You'd better not do it," Kevin warned, and Jack nodded in agreement.

"I have to do a demo with Sean now. You can come and watch if you want."

"Yes, we'll watch. Master Cleary is in a meeting with some Doms."

As soon as he approached Sean, he put up his hand like a stop sign. A painful lump lodged in Brett's throat. It had all gone terribly wrong; Sean had given him an opportunity to become his sub and he had walked away. It wasn't how he had imagined he would have reacted, but the gruesome circumstances sucked. Sean was right; he either trusted him or he didn't. The problem was Sean changed daily. Some days he trusted him and other days he feared him.

"Are you going to work at becoming my sub?" Sean's eyes had a hint of fire in them, then he winked.

"I'm here to work with you now."

"That's not my question."

"I'm not doing it unless I get some money upfront and we do a practice run."

"I can arrange that." Sean dug his wallet out and handed him a hundred euros. "Now will you do it?"

First, Brett counted the money and made sure the bills weren't counterfeit. Once he was satisfied, he nodded and stuffed them into his wallet.

"Words, Brett. I need your verbal agreement."

"Yes, I'll do it."

"Why are your friends in the audience?"

"I guess they want to see you work with me."

"Somehow, I think it's more than that. I don't want you fucking around on me."

Brett shook his head. "Does that only apply to me or are you included in not messing around?"

"I'm going to discipline you later. I make the rules and you follow them. We're going to practice for the roasting competition."

"Are you trying me out to see if you really want to collar me after you told me so many times you didn't?"

The word roasting made Brett cringe with horror. If he could get past the day of the roasting, he'd have money and Sean's collar. Or would he be burned alive without either? A part of him believed Sean and another part didn't. How would he know which Sean would show up for the roasting competition? Was he filling in all the details? He needed to talk to the other subs who were going to enter and see if they'd ever experienced it.

"We need to begin the scene now. Follow my directions or I'll make you regret it," Sean whispered in his ear.

Brett hated to be humiliated in public and Sean knew that, but it never changed the way he dealt with Brett.

"Remove your shorts."

Brett unzipped his leather shorts and put them on a chair. He wore the underwear Sean had gotten him for this scene. The Peek-A-Boo backside, open boxer shorts were sexy, showing off a bit of his ass cheeks. Sean had purchased him black mesh ones, which pushed Brett to agree to be somewhat naked in front of everyone. He might as well get used to it since he wanted to win the competition.

"Tonight, I'm going to demonstrate how to get your sub ready for play. Brett is going to be my model sub for the evening and maybe longer. As most of you know, it's the sub who makes the final decisions. First, I'm going to take care of his nips. Remove the vest!"

Brett slipped his vest off and placed it on top of his leather shorts. He faced Sean, who pinched each pink nipple. The feeling went straight to the base of his cock. He had to keep it down, but Sean twisted them until Brett jerked from pain and pleasure. Sean winked at him.

"I'm going to use some nip clamps. You can get them here in the gift store. If you want different ones, you can order them online. I have two types here. The first set is clothespins." He held them up so everyone could see them. "I'm going to try these out on Brett. Are you ready?"

"Yes, sir."

Sean squeezed his nipple until it turned red, then he clipped on the clothespin. After the initial sharp pain, Brett enjoyed the sensation. Sean pinched the other nipple while Brett held in his breath to ride the pain. Within seconds, Sean clipped the other one.

"Do you like these?"

"Yes, sir."

Sean took another set of nipple clamps and held them up so everyone could see them. "These nipple clamps have bells on them if you want to know where your sub is in the house. You can adjust how tight you want them to be by turning the screws tighter on each clamp. Always check to see if your sub is okay with the level of pain. Loosen it if your sub tells you it's too tight."

Sean removed the clothespins one at a time, and Brett felt the extreme burn.

"When you remove the clamps or clothespins, they will feel an intense burning."

Sean put on a nip clamp and screwed it tight. Very tight. Then he did the other one. The pain was nearly intolerable. Brett allowed the pain to travel and his cock hardened. The tip of the head appeared above his waistband.

"These clamps can be placed on the balls and cock too. You could cover their body with them. I'm going to show you how to put a cock cage on. Are you ready, Brett?"

"Yes, sir."

Brett lifted his head and gazed into Sean's eyes like he was drunk on love and pleasure/pain. Sean held the metal-ringed cock cage in his hand.

"Good boy. I'm going to put this cock cage on you. I'm the only one that can unlock it. I'll take it off after the demonstration. I'll keep the key to this around my neck."

"Yes, sir."

"It has five metal rings with leather holding them together. The first ring will go around your balls, the other four go around your cock. This cock cage isn't as bad as it looks. You won't make a mess when you piss." Sean winked. The men in the audience laughed and some clapped.

"Any questions before I put the cage on Brett?"

Sean pointed to someone who had their hand raised.

"Did you ever lose the key?"

"Absolutely not."

"Why would you put that on a sub?" a man shouted out.

"Many reasons. It can be used as a punishment, or when you do edge play then allow the sub to come only when you want him to. You can't get hard with one on. That's the point."

Sean pulled his mesh underwear to his knees and there stood Brett with a full erection.

"In cases when the sub has an erection, you can't put the cage on. So, I use ice to get rid of the hard-on." Sean took a thermos of ice and poured out a few cubes. He ran them up and down Brett's erection then he ran one cube under his balls. His erection disappeared. "Good boy."

Sean slipped the first cold ring around Brett's cock to the base of his balls and then he pushed his cock through the rest of the rings. He clicked the lock shut, then pulled up Brett's mesh underwear.

"Another thing you can do is insert a butt plug to get him ready." He picked up a glass butt plug. He wiped it down with lube.

"Bend over the table."

Once Brett was in position, Sean pulled his mesh underwear down and lubed his opening. He took the butt plug and slipped it inside. It was cold and uncomfortable. He pulled up his mesh underpants once more.

"He's ready to play. Thank you for attending the demonstration tonight."

Chapter 6

Sean removed the key around his neck for the cock cage and dangled it in front of Brett. "Maybe I should keep that on you, so you stay out of trouble."

"That's not funny. Take it off," Brett demanded.

"That's not how a sub speaks to any Dom whether it's his Dom or someone else's. Don't you raise your voice to me ever again. You have a lot to learn."

"I want this cage off, Sean." Brett shot Sean a death glare.

Sean's smile was cold and cruel like he was. He was doing another flip because his peers weren't watching his behavior. He drove Brett insane when he teased him beyond his endurance. He was always pushing him.

"We need to talk in the van now, so I'll remove it then."

"What about the butt plug and nipple clamps?"

"It would do you some good to walk with them. Just put on your vest and shorts."

"I'll take these off myself." Brett reached for his nipple clamp.

Sean stopped him. "No. I told you I'll remove them at the van. Your disrespectful behavior is why no Dom wants you. All you do is complain and try to change the rules."

"Rules? What rules? I guess everything you said about the sub being in control was just rubbish." Brett zipped up his leather shorts and slipped into his vest. He looked absolutely ridiculous walking around with visible nipple clamps and a butt plug up his ass. No one could see the cock cage, but he wanted it off. Damn Sean. He was always taking him to the brink of absurdity and insanity.

"Follow me, boy, or you'll sleep with that cage on."

Brett wanted to scream at Sean, but he held the key to his release. Sean turned around and pulled a leash from his bag of toys. He put the collar on and attached the leash.

"Why did you put that collar on me?"

"Because you're mine for the rest of the weekend. That's what you want. I might as well make sure no one collars you here."

"Sean, I guess you were lying to me in Dublin. You said I could find a Dom here, and now you're making it so I can't."

"You have me." Sean flashed him a cocky grin.

"No, I don't. You just tease me until I hate you."

"If you don't shut your mouth, I'll tape it shut," Sean snapped and grabbed him by the face.

Where was Master Cleary when he needed him? He thought they were going to the puppy race with a few couples. He wanted to be a puppy in the race, but he needed a Dom to enter. He'd mentioned it to Sean, but he said he had better things to do than to be his foster Dom.

Brett stepped away from Sean. "There's still time to join the puppy race."

"I told you no. Stop begging." Sean turned away, not even trying to hide his annoyance as he checked out a nearly naked sub wearing a collar.

"I'm not." Brett thought Sean looked like he'd dump him for another guy.

They finally entered the campervan, Brett following Sean.

"We need to talk about the competition scene. I need to give you all the facts so you're good with it. I can just as easily ask the boy I had here today, but I'd rather have you."

"I'm not talking about that until you remove this cock cage."

"What if I flush the key down the toilet?" Sean flashed his famous I-got-you-by-the-balls grin.

"I'm leaving. Master Cleary will let me stay with them."

"Come here. I'm just playing with you." He unzipped Brett's shorts and shoved them down along with his underwear. He unlocked the cock cage and rubbed Brett's cock. "Such a beautiful cock."

Sean twisted Brett's clamps then unscrewed one until it was loose enough to remove. All the blood rushed back into the nipple, the intensity making Brett squirm and exhale to ride the pain.

"Hey, are you okay?"

Brett nodded and waited for the other one to be removed. Sean fiddled with the screw, loosened it, and put it on the side table. Again, the intensity of the blood rushing to his left nipple had Brett panting and bringing moans of pleasure from him. Sean shifted his hands, holding his balls while pulling his foreskin back as far as possible. The pain and pleasure caused Brett to moan in delight. He spread his legs wider, allowing Sean fuller access. Sean rubbed his cock until Brett exploded in his hand. Brett had mixed feelings, needing to come but wanting Sean to use his cock instead of his damn hand. Brett had failed to graduate to Sean using his dick to fuck him.

Sean stopped him before he entered the shower, removed Brett's collar and leash, and stored them under the bed in a basket.

Brett stepped into the bathroom and removed his butt plug. He rinsed it with soap and water, then he showered. Sean's words of love were unspoken or nonexistent. Sean got him off because he felt obligated, but that wasn't how he wanted to come.

He dried himself and found another pair of leather shorts and a vest. This time no underwear. He wrapped a bandana around his head. He found Sean with a beer in his hand.

"Where do you think you're going dressed like that?"

"Looking for a decent Dom." Brett needed to be alone, away from Sean.

"We need to talk. That's why we're here."

"About what? You lie to me, and I buy it because you're a Dom. I didn't realize Doms could be liars."

Sean inched closer to him. "Are you calling me a liar, boy?"

"What else is it when you say one thing and do another?"

"Maybe changing my mind on something. Don't think it's okay to disrespect me like that. Next time, I'll beat your ass."

"Sorry, Sean." Brett's cock stirred with thoughts of Sean beating his ass until he traveled to subspace. Why did he have to be so hot looking?

"Just watch how you talk to me. Listen to what I have to say. See if you want to accept my terms for our new arrangement."

"You don't care about me. I mean, you gave me a gentleman's hand job. That's all you've got for me. You fuck tons of guys, but not me. Why?"

"That's why we need to talk about the why and what I want from you and what you need from me. Could you sit down so we can discuss the terms?"

Brett took a seat.

"I know more about you than you do. If I fucked you, you would want to marry me. I know how you are. You're possessive and jealous."

"So why are we talking if I'm not what you want?"

"I think we could work well together. You've grown on me, especially on this trip. I like you at my side. I need a sub and you need a Dom. We could do special competitions for this rich man to earn money, but I need a good sub who I can trust."

"I need to know more about that roasting scene."

"Let's take a walk to where they have the cages set up. You can check it out."

"Now?"

"It's still light out. You need to see it, so you don't create scary images in your head."

"I'll change into my jeans."

"No, you look cute like that." Sean's gaze dropped from his eyes to his shoulders to his cock.

Brett bit his lip to stifle the outcry of delight. Sean made no attempt to hide the fact he was checking him out. He appraised Brett with more than mild interest. Something had changed between them, but Brett feared trusting it would bring him great sadness and loss. Brett was puzzled and more than a little nervous.

They left the campervan and hiked along the grass path. Suddenly, Sean was excited to show him something. Brett wished Sean had been excited about showing him demos in the main hall.

Sean stopped and pointed to the three cages hung between tall trees. Each cage was set at the same height about five feet above the makeshift fire areas. Stones surrounded the firepits. The wire cages didn't look comfortable especially if he was naked.

"What do you think of it?"

"I don't know."

"You know how you wanted me to be your Dom?"

"I used to until you fucked around with all those guys this week."

"Get over it. Things are turning in your favor. Do you want to try out the cage?"

"I don't want my leather shorts and vest to get ruined."

"Simple solution. Take them off."

"Are you going to keep the door open?"

"Whatever you want."

Hopefully he could see how it felt before he decided. He needed the money if he wanted to move to Galway.

"If I want to get out, are you going to help me?"

"Yes. Learn to trust me. Things might work out between us."

Brett unzipped his shorts, shoved them to his ankles, and stepped out of them. Now he wished he had worn underwear. He slipped off his vest.

"Looking good, Brett!"

"Thanks."

Brett walked over to the wire cage and opened the door.

"Hey, I'll get you in there." Sean picked Brett up and slid him headfirst towards the right side. He assisted Brett in moving his legs inside. Sean tied some rope around Brett's wrists and to the wire cage, then he roped his ankles to each side. The wire dug into his skin. "The rich man had his man set it up for us to practice. This cage has been treated with a fireproof coating and is heat resistant. His kink is getting off on frightened subs. He's willing to pay a mighty price for his desires."

"It's not very comfortable in here."

"It's almost like roasting a pig."

Brett didn't like knowing that these cages were going roast subs over fires. Comparing him to a pig repulsed him.

"I bought you fire-resistant underpants for the day of the competition. You must protect your jewels."

"I don't know if I can be in here when there's a fire."

Sean untied Brett, then leaned inside and helped him out.

"Good job, Brett. You did very well." Sean ignored Brett's concerns as always. If he would just once show he cared by his words or actions, but Brett never felt it.

"Thanks. I'm not sure about this. I need more time to think about it."

"Don't think too long. Many subs would love for me to collar them, but then, you know that."

Chapter 7

Sean was gone when Brett woke up. He said he had to meet with the two other Doms involved in the competition. After he dressed in his jeans and T-shirt, his phone buzzed with a new message. Before he looked to see who, he hoped Sean had changed his mind and would take him to the coupled Dom and sub luncheon. Brett picked up his phone. He was disappointed with Sean for acting the same old way of ignoring his requests, and shocked to see Master Cleary had sent him a message.

Master Cleary: *Come to my campervan now. I need to speak to you.*

Brett: *OTW, sir.* He left after he returned the message.

He couldn't imagine what Master Cleary wanted to talk to him about. Had Kevin and Jack told him about what he planned to do for money? He thought they were his friends. Master Cleary would approve of the competition if it was safe, sane, and consensual, but if it were then why wasn't the competition approved by the BDSM camp?

Brett knocked on Master Cleary's door and he answered it with a concerned look. That particular expression worried Brett. Had he done something wrong, and was he going to tell him not to associate with Kevin and Jack? Of course, they must have told him about the scene. That had to be it.

"Come in and sit down."

Brett sat at the tiny table with him and scanned the inside for Jack and Kevin. They were gone.

"Tell me what you know about Sean," Master Cleary said.

"He was a customer where I used to work. I told him what was going on at my job and he helped me move and get a job in Dublin at a bar."

"Did you know he was a Dom?"

"Yes. He told me right off."

"Did you know Colin knows Sean?"

"No. I never saw him talk to him."

"Colin has been kicked out of a few BDSM clubs. He has a bad reputation. He abuses subs like he did with you. I'm worried Sean may be part of Colin's imposter group. They are fake Doms. You need to be careful with Sean."

"Do you think Sean is part of the imposter Dom group?"

"I don't know. If he asks you to do something you don't want to do and he refuses to let you out of it, leave him."

"I will, sir. I told Sean about Colin, and he didn't mention he knew him."

"That says a lot about Sean. Remember if you find yourself in trouble, call me. I'll come and get you if you can't get to me."

"I will, sir. Did Jack or Kevin tell you I was going to enter a competition?"

"What competition?"

"I thought they might have said something. Sean wants me to be his partner in a competition. He said if we win, he'll collar me."

"Collar you? After he fucked all those guys and kicked you out of the camper?" Master Cleary asked.

"I asked him about that. He said I was too jealous and clingy, so he didn't want me."

"And you believe he wants you now?"

"I think he does. I'm not sure."

"Do not take his collar unless you are one hundred percent sure. I don't trust he has your best interests at heart. I know you want a Dom, and you'll get one in good time."

"Thanks for talking to me."

"What kind of scene does he want you to do?"

"I'm not allowed to tell you. I'm sorry, but I don't want him pissed off."

"Remember when you decide if you're going to do the scene, you are allowed to use your safeword. It must be safe, sane, and you must consent to the scene. If you don't feel safe doing it, then don't. If you think it's a crazy scene, don't do it. If you are consenting so he collars you, don't do it. No Dom would give you conditions before they collar you."

"I'll remember that, sir."

"Remember if you need help, call me."

"Yes, sir."

Later in the day, he met up with Kevin and Jack. They were outside eating chocolate ice cream cones on a bench. He went over to them.

"Hey, where did you get the ice cream?"

"Inside. Next to the gift shop there's an ice cream stand," Jack said.

"Master Cleary wanted to talk to me today."

"Yes, he told us. He wanted to talk to you about that man who cuffed you," Kevin said.

"Did you mention the competition?" Jack asked.

"I told him about it, but not the details. Please don't tell him."

"You said you weren't going to do it. Did you change your mind?" Kevin asked.

"I don't know if I will or won't do it. Sean said he wants to collar me."

"Only if you do that insane scene with fire. That's not how real Doms operate. We know. We had one who lied to us and did everything opposite of what he was supposed to do. We don't want you to do anything with Sean," Kevin said.

"You could get burned and have permanent scarring. Don't do it," Jack begged.

Brett heard what they said, and their words and expressions freaked him out. Brett was bad at accepting feedback. He'd had a near miss when he had worked for Mr. Bailey. After helping him once, Mr. Bailey had turned into a pimp and Brett had owed him. He didn't want to be used by men, so Mr. Bailey agreed to be paid his cut from the men Brett served. After the first time, he reached out to Sean for advice and Sean helped him escape the job. For that help, he would be grateful to Sean for the rest of his life.

"I need to meet Sean. See you around later."

Both looked at him as if they would never see him again. Their expressions frightened and worried him. They could be right, and he could be making the biggest mistake of his life. He wanted a Dom, and it didn't matter who at this point. He had to get experience.

Brett walked to Sean's booth. He was closing his area.

"Why are you packing up?"

"We're done here. Tomorrow, we have the competition, then we leave for Dublin. We both have to get back to work."

"I guess we do." Brett helped Sean pack.

"Those Doms and their subs are going to meet us where we set the cages. You can talk to the two other subs. I thought it would help."

Sean seemed friendly enough as they walked along the path with their few bags to the van and dropped them off.

"Are you sure this is safe for me?" Brett asked.

"Don't you trust me? It doesn't sound like it. I planned to give you your collar tonight, so you are my sub."

"What will that mean to you?"

"It means I'm going to teach you how to behave as my sub, not remain the bratty spoiled boy."

"Is that how you see me?"

"At work you flirt and that will stop once you are collared."

Brett almost didn't want to be collared by Sean. He made it sound like he was going to control every facet of his life. He wanted to know if Sean knew Colin and if he did, why hadn't he mentioned it when he told him what he had done.

"Is something wrong, Brett?"

"Do you know Colin?"

"Who told you I knew him?"

"So, you do know him, but you didn't mention it?"

"Who told you I know him?" Sean asked.

"I heard Colin isn't a Dom and he was kicked out of here."

"He's a Dom. Did your Master Cleary tell you he wasn't?" He shouted at Brett with fury on his face. Sean's words hurt just as he meant them to.

"Is he a Dom or not?" Brett shouted back.

"Yes. There are different kinds of Doms as there are subs. Not all fit in the same pair of jeans. So, yes, he is. You know I am because we go to the BDSM club, or did you forget?"

"I don't really get why all of a sudden you want to collar me?"

"Are you changing your mind?"

"About what?"

"Did your Master Cleary talk you out of being my sub?"

"I make my own decisions. I've wanted you to pay attention to me, like maybe fuck me when we travel together instead of you fucking everyone else in sight except me."

"Is that what this is about?"

"It's about you wanting me and not others. I can't share my Dom. I really wanted you, but this weekend kind of turned me off."

"See, I knew you were possessive, but if and when I collar you, you and I will be the only two fucking."

Chapter 8

Sean and Brett left to meet the other Doms and subs entering the competition. Once they got there, Brett's stomach turned over each time he looked at the cages. Two men, one who looked familiar, were standing by one of the cages.

"Hey, Sean. This is Pat, my sub. Is that Brett?"

"Brett, this is Master John, and his sub, Pat. Brett is going to be my sub very soon."

"That's great news. I want Pat and Brett to talk alone while we discuss some of the details," Master John said.

"Have you done this before?" Brett asked Pat.

"I did it when we practiced a few times. It looks worse than it really is."

"Did you get burned anywhere?"

"No. There was a little fire under the cage. What is tough is the constant spinning of the rotisserie unit from the generator. I got dizzy and sick with the heat of the fire."

"Did you use your safeword to stop?"

"Yes, I had to, or I'd have thrown up. When are you getting collared?"

"I don't know. He said after I do this scene. That is, if I do good."

"How long have you been with Sean?"

"Two years. We work together at Murphy's Pub."

"So, he's played with you for two years and you're still not collared?"

"He's played with me a few times. He wasn't interested in me until now."

"Do you trust him?"

"Sometimes."

"I always trusted Master John. He has been good for me. Make sure you really want Sean's collar."

"Have you ever met Sean before?" Brett asked.

"No."

"Do you know who the other Dom and sub are?"

"No. Master John met Sean in Dublin when he was on a business trip."

"Oh. He never mentioned it."

"He met Sean in the pub you both work in."

"Oh, I thought he looked familiar."

"Are you nervous about tomorrow?"

"I'm afraid of getting burned alive."

"Listen. If you don't trust Sean to keep you from burning, Master John will make sure you're safe. I hope that helps a little."

"So you think it's safe?" Brett asked again, not believing him. He didn't know who to believe or what he should do about the scene. If he did it with Sean, he'd collar him. As much as he wanted to be collared, things between them changed when Sean messed around with those other guys. He kept telling himself Sean wanted to be friends, but the problem was Brett wanted more than that. Or he did until this camp trip and all the guys Sean had fucked.

"It's safe, but if you don't feel comfortable with the scene, don't do it and don't accept Sean's collar. If you can't trust him, he's the wrong Dom for you."

"I just wanted to get some experience with serving a Dom."

"Wait until you meet the right Dom. You'll know. It will feel right."

"I'll think about it."

Sean interrupted their conversation. "Hey, we're going to do a quick run, so you'll feel safe."

Brett had so many conflicting feelings. His priority was to get a Dom. If Sean collared him, then he'd get experience. If it was the only way to get his collar, he'd do the scene. He walked to the cage.

"Get naked boys," Master John said.

Both Brett and Pat undressed and stood side by side.

"Brett, you're not going in until I protect your dick." Sean wrapped a leather sack around his balls and dick then handed him fireproof underwear.

Master John did the same for Pat. Pat was all smiles like he had done it several times. The trust he had for his Dom was not the same as the lack of trust Brett felt at times for Sean.

"Now, let me help you into the cage. This time I'm going to lock the door." Brett trembled as Sean helped him inside. He tied his limbs to the cage the same way Master John had done to Pat.

Brett could see Pat smiling in his cage. Without notice, Master John and Sean collected dead branches and placed them in a circle under their cages. Brett wasn't told there would be a fire during practice. Of course, Sean had lied or as he would say he "left out" some details. If he got burned, it would be Sean's fault for not taking care of him.

Once they both had their firewood, Master John nodded to Sean. He pulled out a lighter and started the fire going underneath him. The crackling of the fire worried him. The warmth of the fire reached his body. Beads of sweat rolled down his face.

"Let's turn on the generator and the rotisserie unit and roast those boys," Sean said.

"Ready, Pat?" Master John asked.

"Yes, sir."

"Brett, are you ready?" Sean asked.

"Yes, sir." Was he supposed to get turned on spinning over an open fire? The flames remained low, but once they turned them on, both cages began spinning at a slow pace. Between the heat and spinning, Brett's stomach rebelled. Pain filled his head. He had to get out of this damn cage. He managed to grin through the pain like Pat. He didn't look worried. His expression looked like he had floated into subspace. The flame grew closer.

"Sean! The fire!" Brett yelled.

Sean quickly threw dirt on the fire and turned off the spinning. He opened the cage and helped him out. "You okay?"

Brett shook his head. "I feel sick to my stomach."

By the time Sean had him untied, Pat stood outside his cage as if it was nothing to him.

"Hey, Sean. I think we need to go to plan B tomorrow night," Master John said.

"Agreed." Sean turned to Brett. "I'll meet you back at the van. I need to talk to John privately." He pulled a bottle of water from his backpack and handed it to Brett.

Brett quickly dressed. Sean didn't seem to care what he did since he was talking to Master John. Brett picked up some speed along the path. He tripped on a log, knocking the wind out of himself. When he looked up, the trees were spinning, or he was. He forced himself up, leaning on a tree. He pushed forward by grabbing onto one tree then another. He found a mossy spot and lay there with his eyes closed.

Sean didn't give a damn about him. His lack of nurturing disturbed him more with this scene than at other times. Sean knew how frightened and uneasy he was about the scene. He practically threw the bottle of water right at him.

Master John gave Pat a candy bar, water, and hugs. They cared about each other the way Brett needed, but Sean wasn't going to give him what he needed. The sex left much to be desired, that is, if you could call it sex.

Tears ran down his face; he hated his lonely miserable life. He needed someone to take care of him. Sounds of someone walking nearby interrupted his morbid thoughts. Maybe it was Sean thinking he needed to check on him. Sean needed to read a book on aftercare.

"Brett, are you okay?" Master Cleary asked.

"Not doing great." Brett looked up at him. Sometimes, Master Cleary appeared out of nowhere like he had been assigned to be his guardian angel.

"How can I help?" Master Cleary stooped beside him.

"I have to make a decision about Sean. I've wanted him to be my Dom since we met. Finally, he gave me a way to get his collar. He's helped me out of jams but lately I'm not sure."

"You're in a bad place not having family so you need someone, but it has to be someone who will care for you. With Kevin and Jack, I wanted them happy, and I'd figured out they could not be split up. I took them both, and now I can't imagine living without either of them. Tell me what you like about Sean?"

"It's not the sex because there's no sex." Brett fisted his tears away.

"Why won't he have sex with you?"

"I guess I'm too ugly and stupid."

"That's not true at all. You're very handsome and I like you as a person. I don't think you're stupid. You had to fight for your survival from the time you were a child. That's tough."

The more Master Cleary spoke about him, the more tears came. Breaking down in front of anyone was something he'd always tried to prevent.

"I'm sorry I'm a mess. I didn't mean to get you mixed up in my drama."

"You didn't do anything wrong. Remember whatever you decide doesn't necessarily mean it's permanent. Every single mistake can be corrected. What I'm saying is if you decide to be Sean's sub and later you feel unhappy and uncomfortable, you can leave. Call me if you need help."

"Thanks. I'm going to think about it later."

As soon as Master Cleary walked away, Sean came out of nowhere. "Brett! Let's go. I thought you'd be at the campervan by now."

Brett had no idea what to say, so he lifted one shoulder in a half shrug and followed Sean to the van. He didn't want to cause any problems.

Chapter 9

As soon as they entered the campervan, Brett undressed and went to the bed they had shared on the trip. He had a lot to think about before he ruined his life. It had never occurred to him he could leave if Sean mistreated him in any way.

"Hey, are you okay?" Sean pulled off his shirt.

"Just tired that's all."

Sean grabbed two beers and handed one to Brett. "We need to talk."

"About what now?"

"Andy called. It wasn't good either. He knows you're with me."

Brett sat up in bed and sipped his beer. "What did he say?"

"He told me to tell you not to come in anymore." Sean unraveled the label from the beer bottle.

"Why? What did I do wrong? And why did he call you?" He gulped his beer.

"He fired you. You know Andy's boyfriend wanted your job and Andy didn't want to speak to you."

"He can't fire me for no reason."

"He owns the pub, and he can hire and fire anyone he wants."

"What was the reason he told you?"

"He said the drawer was short three hundred euros on your last night. He said he warned you about this before."

"I didn't take three hundred euros from him."

"Andy's boyfriend set you up. I bet he took the money so Andy would fire you."

"What am I going to do now? Can't you fix it?"

"There's nothing to fix. You need to get another job, but not in Dublin. Andy will blackball you there. You need to move."

"And go where?"

"Why not Galway? You love it here. I can help you move."

"Move? So, I guess you lied about giving me a collar."

"No. If you win tomorrow, I'll collar you and we'll both move."

"Did Andy fire you too?"

"No. Well, not yet. He probably will."

Again, Sean was selling his collar if he performed well and won the competition. He could do the scene and depending on Sean's behavior towards him, he could say no, but then he would need him to move here and help him find a job. Sean had helped him move and get a job before so based on the past, he would be good for that. All this hung on Brett doing the scene he didn't want to do.

"What if we win the competition and you still have a job at Murphy's, what would you do?"

"If we win, I'll collar you and we'll move. We could get new jobs."

Brett wanted to believe Sean, but he rarely kept his word on certain things.

"What's wrong, Brett? I know that look."

"Are you ever going to fuck me, or do I have to earn that?"

"Are you saying you want to try out the merchandise first?"

"I'm not sure you're sexually attracted to me. Why else won't you fuck me?"

Sean rushed to the bed and pulled off the covers. Brett wondered if he really would fuck him. As he shoved his underwear down, he kicked them to the side of the bed. Sean stripped down so fast Brett's head spun. To finally have the man he wanted to fuck him filled him with joy. If only this excitement would last after, he would be so happy he'd be getting experience being a sub. For all he knew Sean had been waiting for the right time. Brett's spirits lifted when Sean crashed on the bed with a condom. He put it on and lubed his huge erection.

"Do you want a blindfold?"

Brett nodded.

"I figured you did." He got up and pulled out a wooden paddle and a black leather blindfold from the basket under the bed. He climbed back onto the bed and tied the blindfold over Brett's eyes.

The blindfold was lined with soft black fleece for extra comfort. The fleece blocked light more effectively than other padding. Sean told him this was his favorite blindfold, and he'd used it on Brett before. Hopefully that meant he was special to Sean after all.

"Wait, I owe you a spanking over my knee first."

Brett laughed. "For what?"

"You know how disrespectful you have been to me. Now, I can spank you because I don't fuck unless I spank first." He sat on the edge of the bed and helped Brett fall across his lap.

"Are we doing a scene?" Brett wondered if he needed to use his safeword.

"No, this is Sean fucking Brett. It's been a long time coming. No safewords."

Sean raised his hand and brought it smartly down on Brett's bare ass. He jumped, but it didn't really hurt, it had just taken him by surprise. Sean spanked him again, and Brett's cock grew stiff.

"I've wanted to do this for a long time," Sean said.

Brett imagined what he looked like over Sean's knee, with both of them naked. The staccato rhythm of his spanking hand provided much-needed heat, making his cock stiffen even more. He prayed he didn't squirt down Sean's leg.

"Damn," Sean said. "My hand is really getting sore. Luckily, I have the wooden paddle." Sean lifted the paddle from the bed and brought it crashing down on Brett's ass. He heard it before he felt it. The force behind the paddle propelled Brett forward a couple of centimeters across Sean's lap. Sean landed the paddle on his ass a few more times.

"Fuck! That's too hard." Brett's stomach was busy turning inside out. His hands were sweaty.

"Language, boy."

He swung even harder this time. Brett was surprised at how fast and hard he swung the paddle before it crashed on his poor bottom. These swats were personal, nothing like when they had done a scene. This was Sean touching him, skin to skin. Brett didn't have to wait long for the next, nor for the remaining ones. They landed in a steady rhythm, each as hard as the first.

Now that stung! Brett gritted his teeth and waited for the next. The pain intensified with each and Brett embraced every flare.

"Too bad you can't see how red your ass is, and the redder it gets, the harder my cock gets."

"Feels good." Brett couldn't figure out why Sean had waited so long to fuck him with his cock. He certainly would have consented from day one.

Suddenly a flash of pain swiped across his bared bottom as he tensed up. Shortly after, another one. Brett gritted his teeth, not wanting to cry out in front of Sean. A few moments later, another stroke. Brett knew he couldn't hold back tears.

"The paddle is too mild for punishment, but tonight is more about getting both of us ready so I can fuck you."

"Please fuck me," Brett begged.

"Get on your hands and knees on the bed." Sean helped Brett onto the bed and into position since he wore the blindfold. Brett heard Sean rip open a condom. He lined up behind Brett and aimed for his target. Sean pierced the ring of Brett's opening and bottomed out inside of him with one quick push. He was grateful Sean took the time to lube both of them.

"Should have fucked you when I met you."

"Told you." Brett laughed.

Sean pinched his nipple enhancing his already incredibly turned-on state; he'd lusted for Sean from the moment he'd met him.

"Your asshole is tight."

"I probably needed some stretching." Brett's dick wasn't complaining.

Sean wrapped his hand around Brett's pulsating hard-on, caressing it at the same tempo he pumped in and out. Brett trembled, tightening his anal muscles around the hard cock banging deep inside him. The warm semen in his balls threatened to shoot, and he couldn't fight much longer as his body quivered, trying to hold back the climax that was ready.

"I'm going to come," Brett said.

"Wait. Wait for me," Sean shouted.

"Too late." Brett's balls throbbed, begging to release. Sean's painful grip on the base of Brett's cock cut off the flow, allowing only a small dribble to escape.

"Wait," Sean repeated.

Sean rode him harder, forcing Brett to shoot his cum all over his hand and on the sheets.

"Keep fucking me," Brett begged, riding the path of pleasure.

"Oh, fuck. Fuck. I can't stop it. Oh, fuck."

Brett pushed his ass toward the cock thrashing inside him. As Sean's warm cum exploded, both moaned and collapsed on the bed facing each other.

"You were a lot better than I thought," Sean whispered.

"I figured you were good." Brett had seen the size of Sean's dick and had wanted to be fucked with it.

"I'm the best in bed, but I suck at aftercare. I saw you watch John with Pat. I guess I could learn more."

"Did you ever think that maybe Master John loves Pat? It comes easy for them."

"The thought never crossed my mind. Are you going to be okay tomorrow?"

"Are you going to make sure I'm safe from the fire?"

"I want you to wear my collar tomorrow."

"What would it mean?"

"It means you're my sub for the competition and when we win, you'll be my real sub if you agree to follow my rules, which we haven't discussed yet."

Brett wondered if all this was about money. What he needed to know was if you had to have a sub to enter. Was this fucking all about Sean wanting to win the competition for money? He got a sick feeling in his stomach.

The fucking was good, but Sean wasn't affectionate enough. The other Doms who had sex with Brett acted like they cared, but there were many who wouldn't have sex with him. He'd had more sex when he worked for Mr. Bailey but then Mr. Bailey ruined the job by pimping him out.

"I'm going to rinse off and have a cigarette outside. Be right back."

Brett watched Sean wash and dress. Once he left, he'd probably take a walk and wouldn't return until Brett was asleep.

Chapter 10

Sean sat on the edge of the bed and woke Brett from a deep sleep. He rubbed his eyes with the base of his palms. Brett remained quiet, staring at Sean blankly. He handed him a cup of coffee. It was the first time Sean had served Brett in bed or anywhere else. Sean demanded Brett serve him, not because he was his Dom either. He told him his job was to always respect him and all Doms if he desired to be a good sub. Brett had bought into his submissive position when it came to Sean. He passed it off as gaining sub experience.

"I figured you needed coffee. We have a full day. After the competition, we need to leave for Dublin."

"Because you have to work?" Brett sipped his hot coffee. It tasted wonderful. Sean had laced it with just the right amount of sugar. Brett was surprised Sean had known how much sugar he used. He reminded himself, this was the Sean who wanted something from him, not the one who cared.

"I don't think my job is secure since we're friends. We probably need to pack up and move to Galway. There are tons of places here where we can get a job."

"Where will we stay until we get jobs?"

"Cheap hotels or we could camp if we run out of money."

"I hope you're not just slagging me."

Sean leaned towards him and hugged him. "Trust me. Remember I helped you move to Dublin and got you the job? I won't leave you homeless, not after what you've been through. Take a shower and get dressed."

"Where are you going?"

"Outside to smoke, then we'll have breakfast at the Mess Hall." Sean lifted Brett's chin and claimed his mouth with a savage kiss.

The kiss left Brett off balance, the first one from Sean. Sean always said he hated kissing. The kiss had been a long time coming, and everything Brett had hoped for, but did Sean mean it? His father was right, he was too ugly, and he would live a lonely miserable life. If he could only get out of his own head and take things as they seemed and add nothing else to them. He created his own suffering, and he didn't need to pull shit up from his past to make himself hurt more.

After Sean left the van, Brett quickly showered and dressed wearing a pair of skimpy jeans and a navy T-shirt with the logo of where he had worked. Sadly, he was out of a job. Andy had hurt him when he told him he didn't want to see him anymore. If that wasn't bad enough, his ex-lover had fired him so his new boyfriend could take his job. Sean had been right when he'd told him not to mess around with Andy.

He met Sean outside. Brett figured he would have left without him. That was his usual MO.

"You look sexy today. Come here."

Brett was too frightened to be happy about Sean's collar. There was the possibility of losing and they would return to what they were to each other. Just friends without sex.

Sean pulled out his collar and clasped it. "You're my sub while we're here. That means no messing around."

"I thought we were leaving right after?"

"We are."

Brett rubbed his collar, something he had wanted for so long. Getting attached to it would only bring unhappiness. He should enjoy it while it lasted. Now, he could claim he had a BDSM relationship and was collared. At the Dublin clubs, collaring was a big event, almost like getting married. He had to remember this collar came from Sean, not any other Dom.

"Thanks, Sean."

"When you refer to me, it's Sir or Master Sean."

"Yes, Sir." Brett didn't know if he could call him Master Sean. He wasn't anything like Master Cleary or Dr. Murray.

They walked to the Mess Hall and sat at a table with Master John and Pat. He was glad to see them.

"I see you have your collar," Pat whispered to Brett.

"Yes. He decided he wanted me."

"Nervous about the scene?"

"I'm not looking forward to it."

"Master John told me there will be surprises today but not to worry."

"What does that mean?" A groan accompanied the roll of his eyes. That was the last thing Brett wanted to hear. His spine jumped upright with extreme concern over what was to come at the competition. He still had a chance to drop out of it, but would Sean dump him here?

"They might add some more obstacles for the competition." Pat's face turned red when he got stirred up. Obviously, he looked forward to this crazy event.

"Do you know what they changed or added?"

"No. Master John likes to surprise me. I'm hoping whatever they do, I can reach subspace."

"It sure would make it worth it if we could reach subspace."

"Did you ever reach it with Sean?"

Brett nodded.

A dull headache formed behind his eyes. He glanced around the room and refused to make eye contact with Pat while he gained his bearings. Brett caught Jack's eye across the room. He sat beside Kevin and Master Cleary. Dr. Murray and Aiden were sitting there, too. How he wished he was sitting at their table.

After they were finished, Brett wanted to talk to Master Cleary and the boys. He didn't have a chance because Sean and Master John left from another exit that didn't pass by their table.

"Meet you there, in thirty minutes," Master John said to Sean.

"Where is he meeting you?" Brett asked.

"Not me, us. We need to move the van then walk back."

"Why?"

"After the competition we need to leave."

"Do I have time to say goodbye to my new friends?"

"No."

Brett stopped in the middle of the path to the campervan. "I need to say goodbye if we're leaving."

"Send them a text. We can't be late."

Brett saw red when Sean told him to send a text. He didn't have many friends and the new ones he had made here, he valued. Brett didn't know how he could rectify this intolerable situation. Sean's words and actions were pushing him to hate him. Every time he thought he'd made some forward movement with Sean; it all went to hell.

As they stepped inside the campervan, Sean grabbed two sodas and handed one to Brett.

"Sorry you can't say goodbye to your friends, but we're running out of time. Pack up your things, so when we're back in Dublin, I can turn the campervan in without any holdups. I need to work tonight."

"I didn't know you had to work tonight." Brett had originally thought they were to return to work on Monday; that was until Andy fired him.

"Charlie called in sick."

"I guess Andy didn't fire you."

"I don't trust Andy."

They gathered their clothes and personal items and placed them in their suitcases,

"Sit." Sean pointed to the passenger seat. "We're taking off."

Brett was too nervous to talk while Sean drove out of the camping area to a parking area across the street. They jumped out and hiked down an unfamiliar path.

"Are you going to tell me if you guys changed anything for the competition?"

"You know more than you should. Most subs trust their Doms and don't ask dumb questions. It's all about trust."

"Is this path going to take us to where we practiced?"

"That was just practicing. We needed to change our location because a few more are joining us. The area is all set up for us with dirt to put out the fires. As I said before, if we win, you'll get five hundred euros which we'll split right down the middle, and you'll be my sub."

"I'll do my best to win, but Pat seems like he's done it a million times."

"John and Pat have been together for a few months. He hasn't ever done this before. None of the subs have, just like you."

"Where do they live?" Brett asked, knowing Pat told him during practice he had done it before.

"Galway. We'll probably see them again if we move around here."

"What do you mean if?" Brett tossed him a side-eye.

"Nothing is set in stone. That's what we plan to do."

Brett wondered if Sean would abandon him when they returned to Dublin. He had no idea what he would do if he did. As much as he was uneasy with Sean, he always helped him out of a jam. He needed him one way or another. He had to win today.

Brett froze when they arrived. Brett glared at Master Colin standing beside a young naked sub. Why hadn't anyone told him he'd be here? Then he noticed there was a huge circle of cages propped up by ropes to trees and larger firepits than at the practice area. Each firepit had been filled with sticks. Brett counted ten cages. How would he be able to compete with nine others? He saw lots of guys hanging in small circles talking. All the sub contestants were standing naked beside their Doms.

"I thought we would be early," Sean said. "You okay?"

"Why didn't you tell me Master Colin would be here?" Brett asked.

"I didn't know he was part of this. He won't go near you because you're wearing my collar."

"Are you going to still do it?"

"I need the money, so yes."

"Are you upset the subs are naked?"

"You said I could wear fire resistant underwear."

"You were informed you were going to be mostly naked, or did you forget what you did at practice?"

"Yes, sir. Do you have my fireproof underwear?'

"Yes, in this bag."

"What else is in there?" Brett wondered if they would allow underwear since none of the subs were wearing them.

"It's a surprise. We're at cage four." Sean walked him to their assigned spot.

Master John and a naked Pat were standing in front of cage five.

"Strip down," Sean ordered.

Brett pulled off his T-shirt at a turtle's pace. He handed it across to Sean who placed it into the leather bag. He slipped his boots off, removed his socks, and placed them inside the leather bag. He unzipped his jeans, slid them down, and stepped out of them. He folded them, then put them into the bag.

"My sexy warrior. Wow, you make a good show standing naked there." Sean removed the fireproof underwear from the bag and handed it to him.

"Thanks."

"Wait until they tell you to put them on."

Master John and Pat walked over to them.

"Hey, Brett, how are you doing?" Pat asked.

"Nervous. I know they are going to pull some shit before we get into that cage."

"I overheard another Dom say they were going tie us to a pole. But you should be okay if you don't mind bondage, right?"

"Bondage doesn't bother me, but that fire and spinning..."

"These cages are going to spin faster than the practice ones."

"How do you know that?"

"Look at them. They have a larger generator than the one at practice,"

Brett and Pat listened to what Master John said to Sean. "See that old man sitting on the chair?"

"Who is he?" Sean asked.

"He's the one financing this competition. No one knows his name."

A tall Dom blew a horn and ended their conversation. "Boys, put on your underwear."

"Good luck, Brett," Pat said.

"Good luck to you, too."

Brett quickly stepped into his underwear and pulled them up. At least his jewels would be saved. The thought of roasting over fire didn't turn him on. He didn't understand how ten Doms had convinced ten subs to take part in this insanity. He wanted the entire roasting over with.

Sean threw a long towel on the ground. "Lie face down."

Brett welcomed any time out of the cage. Before he lay flat on the towel, he saw other subs on the ground. Their Doms had rope.

Sean pulled out a red rope. "Get on the towel. Now!"

Brett stooped to the ground then rested face down.

"I'm going to hogtie you, so you stay safe in the cage."

"Sean! You never said we had to be hogtied." Brett panicked.

"We need the money. Just do it."

Sean tied one wrist to one ankle, then did the other one. Once that was done, he slipped a pole across his back, and braided rope around it so he hung from the pole.

"Is it okay?"

"Yes, sir." Brett's eyes watered.

Sean lifted him hanging from the pole and placed him into the cage. The pole slipped inside the ends and locked in place. He could see Pat who looked more concerned than he had before. He hadn't known about being hogtied. Brett shook his head and Pat did the same.

The huge guy took the microphone again and said, "Light the fires. The last sub left wins. Good luck, boys. Use your safewords if you want out."

Brett was locked in the cage as he watched all the Doms light the branches in the fire rings. Smoke turned heavy and Brett felt the heat.

Someone shouted Red; one down, nine to go.

"Turn on the rotisseries, set it on slow." The announcer used the microphone again.

Once the spinning began and the fire grew hotter, Brett's stomach turned. Sweat poured down his face and his eyes burned from the smoke. His body was reddening. He wasn't going to last much longer.

Three other subs shouted Red, leaving six remaining. He didn't want to disappoint Sean. He dry-heaved from the heat as he was spinning.

"Hey, Brett! Are you okay?" Sean asked.

Brett couldn't answer.

"Turn it to medium. Roast those boys," the announcer said.

The faster it went, the sicker Brett felt.

More noise surrounded them as Brett nearly blacked out.

"Put those fires out!" Master Cleary shouted.

Brett was so relieved to hear his voice. He wasn't alone.

"What the fuck is he doing here?" Sean shouted to Brett as he threw a pail of dirt on the fire.

He couldn't answer.

About ten Garda surrounded the Doms and made them remove their subs from the cages. One stepped behind Sean.

"Turn the generator off and get that boy out of that cage."

Sean turned it off, unlocked the door, and helped Brett out. He put Brett on the towel and used his pocketknife to cut the rope to release his limbs. Brett stretched his numb legs and arms.

"I need to see your ID." the Garda ordered.

He issued Sean a ticket. "Leave this camp area and don't ever come back.

Master Cleary rushed over to Sean and Brett.

"What were you thinking?" Master Cleary asked Sean.

"Everything was consensual."

"Consensual my ass. Take your ass out of here and never show your face again."

Brett closed his eyes. Dr. Murray stooped beside Brett. "Hey, are you okay?" He handed Brett a bottle of water.

"Thanks."

Sean lifted Brett over his shoulder and grabbed the leather bag. Brett saw two Garda arresting Master Colin, but the old man sitting in the chair vanished.

"Where are you going with Brett?" Master Cleary asked.

"None of your business. He's my sub." Sean carried him over his shoulder while he ran to the van. Brett didn't know what was going on.

Sean took Brett into the van and put him on the bed. "I think when you feel better you should take a cool shower."

"I'm going to sleep."

"We need to move when we get back. Andy sent me a text not long ago and fired me as well. I guess he didn't need me after all."

"Now what?"

"We move."

"And the collar?"

"You didn't win the money."

Brett unfastened his collar and threw it to Sean.

"Collar or no collar, I'm still going to help you move and get a job."

Brett was relieved on many levels because Sean wasn't the right one for him, but he needed him as a friend for right now.

The End

Want to read about Brett finding a new Dom?

Read Broken Trust:

Irish Collar Series Book 1

ABOUT THE AUTHOR

I am from Huntington Beach, Ca. I taught various subjects at a Continuation High School in Los Angeles, California for 27 years. I obtained a Bachelor of Arts Degree in History, Secondary Social Science Credential and a Master's Degree in Secondary Reading and Secondary Education from California State University, Long Beach. I also enrolled in some creative writing classes at UCLA.

CONNECT WITH BRINA BRADY

I would love to hear from my readers, so please drop me a line.
My email address:
mailto:brinabrady@gmail.com
Sign up for my newsletter:
http://brinabrady.bravehost.com/Newspaper
Join my Reader's Group here:
https://www.facebook.com/groups/146904702344189/
Please visit my WordPress Blog here:
http://brinabrady.wordpress.com
Friend me on Facebook here:
https://www.facebook.com/brina.brady.3
Follow me on Twitter here:
https://twitter.com/BrinaBrady
Follow me on BookBub here:
https://www.bookbub.com/authors/brina-brady
Follow me on Pinterest here:
http://www.pinterest.com/brinabrady/
Follow me on Instagram:
https://www.instagram.com/bradybrina/
Check out my TikToK:
http://www.tiktok.com/@brinabrady
Check out my Link Tree:
https://linktr.ee/brinabrady

OTHER BOOKS

RENT ME SERIES 1-5

Rent Me (Book 1)

http://www.amazon.com/Rent-Me-Book-ebook/dp/B00KLNSLBQ/

Russian mobster spanks his rent boy. Ouch!

Rent Boy Brennen wants to belong to his lover Dmitri Dubrovsky. The Russian mobster controls every inch of his life in and out of bed. Brennen works for Dmitri's escort service. His only desire is to please his lover. When Dmitri marries Nika, his lover moves him out of their home to an apartment in Beverly Hills and tells him nothing has changed.

What is Brennen going to do now?

Brennen does not understand his lover's Russian culture not allowing homosexuality. Two different cultures and age difference clash.

Own Me (Book 2)

http://www.amazon.com/dp/B00VDQLDZ6/

Make Me (Book 3)

http://www.amazon.com/dp/B016B6MZZY/

For Me (Book 4)

http://www.amazon.com/Me-Christmas-Story-Rent-ebook/dp/B018PWUVFI/

Find Me (Book 5)

https://www.amazon.com/Find-Me-Rent-Book-ebook/dp/B01MT9S6PD/

BEND OVER SERIES 1-4

Bend Over (Book 1)

http://www.amazon.com/Bend-Over-Book-ebook/dp/B00P2XO5YM/

Runaway 18-year-old Shane O'Rourke is living under the Huntington Beach Pier.

He carries many secrets from his past. Shane wasn't allowed to explore his sexuality when he lived home with his father, The Reverend. His submissive nature and desires had to remain fantasies.

Shane meets a dark stranger on the beach. Julien Callier is a Dom from Martinique and is sixteen years older than Shane. Bad boy Shane wants to win the heart of Julien Callier and become his sub. But does he really understand what Julien expects from his boy?

Julien's heart goes out to this gorgeous boy, and he takes him under his wing, grooming him to be his sub. Julien is determined to let Shane experience the good life, even financing his education, but he's challenged at every turn by Shane's rebellious nature.

When Shane's defiant behavior threatens to come between them for good, Julien has to act fast to teach Shane the meaning of real submission.

Can Julien tame the bad boy? Can Shane give up his old ways of stealing, lying, and using drugs? The playroom is open.

Don't Throw Me Away (Book 2)

http://www.amazon.com/gp/product/B0117VIQW4/

Spanked in the Woodshed (Book 3)

https://www.amazon.com/Spanked-Woodshed-Bend-Over-Book-ebook/dp/B01BOEWBB6

Breaking Roadblocks (Book 4)

https://www.amazon.com/gp/product/B07649W6RF

THE IRISH RUNAWAY SERIES 1-3

The Runaway Gypsy Boy (Book 1)

https://www.amazon.com/Runaway-Gypsy-Boy-Irish-Book-ebook/dp/B01FIFE3Q8/

Twenty-year-old Daniel Serban loses his dancing job and threats of being outed to his family force him to flee Limerick, Ireland. Daniel fears his father and the other gypsy men will force him to marry his betrothed or bring bodily harm to him for being gay.

As chance would have it, he ends up in Cleary's Pub, a gay leather bar in Galway where he meets the grouchy, ginger-bear Ronan O'Riley. Daniel had no idea how much meeting the Dom would transform his life.

Ronan O'Riley has been unable to move on since the death of his sub a year ago, that is

until a troubled gypsy boy steps into Cleary's. Ronan's lonely existence is about to change.

Can Ronan convince Daniel to trust him or will Daniel's fears of his past ruin any chance of a relationship? Unexpected, heated attraction in the barn ignites their relationship to move forward. Though the two men have many of the same dreams, Daniel's secrets, and Ronan's need to gain Daniel's trust are just a few of the many challenges they must overcome if they are to be together.

Master Cleary's Boys (Book 2)
https://www.amazon.com/Master-Clearys-Boys-Irish-Runaway-ebook/dp/ B01M0AF8DR/

Master Braden's Houseboy (Book 3)
https://www.amazon.com/dp/B07HX2HR3G

BURIED SECRETS SERIES
Buried Secrets (Book 1)
https://www.amazon.com/dp/B07MGHSFQS

When Alek Belanov loses his family at four years old, his Russian mobster uncle raises him.

Now, at twenty-two, Alek wants nothing more than to find out who murdered his family and why. After Alek gets out of prison for a crime he didn't commit, his uncle sends him away to the Gay Protection Society, claiming Alek's life is in danger.

Sexy Rafe Escobar is the head of the secret Gay Protection Society, and he chooses Alek as his personal charge. Rafe warns Alek that if he breaks security rules, he will discipline him. Alek has some slip-ups here and there, but he adores his protector and wishes to please him in every way.

Alek quickly finds his place among the other men who seek shelter and those who guard them. What was supposed to be a safe haven becomes a group on the run as security breaches and threats force them to move from town to town.

Is Rafe and Alek's relationship strong enough to withstand the secrets and deceptions of people trying to destroy them?

Taming Emilio (Book 2)

https://www.amazon.com/gp/product/B07TYS81F2

Dante's Discipline (Book 3)

Gang member Dante Medina committed an unforgivable offence against his family, friends, and gang. It was only a matter of time until his homeboys would jump him out of the gang or worse. His life in East Los Angeles as he knew it would end at the age of twenty-four.

His father sent his two older brothers to take him to his aunt's house in Santa Monica. Dante thought his family was working together to save him from the gang, but that wasn't what happened.

Ex-army officer, protector and Dom, James chose to protect Dante. He is warned to never break the security rules and to accept James's decisions at all times, or his punishment will be harsh. Dante happily accepted the rules and consequences of the Gay Protection Society conditions.

Unfortunately, no amount of protection can alter the gang's determination to take Dante down for good.

MOBSTERS' GAY SONS SERIES

Without Respect (Book 1)

https://www.amazon.com/dp/B08J47C4LP/

An Italian mobster raises three sons, but Sal's youngest son, Benito Banetti, is gay. His father would never allow Ben to be in an openly gay relationship. But Ben intends to change that when he finds the man he wants. When it turns out the man Ben's been seeing is a Banetti family enemy, his father gives him an ultimatum. Either he marries his cousin, and all is forgotten, or if he chooses to be with Mishka Chernov, a Russian mobster, he will disown him.

Mishka Chernov took over his family's business out of love and respect for his father; however, he has come to realize he isn't suitable for this top position in the family. Mishka meets a beautiful man at a sleazy bar, and when he finds out who this man is, he still wants him regardless of the problems Ben Banetti would cause his family's business. Mishka wants the same freedom and separation from family business that Ben has.

Without Respect is about two men raised by mob bosses, realizing their families are enemies, but neither is willing to walk away. This story is book one of a MM romance that follows their relationship. It has some D/s and light BDSM elements.

Loyalty Required (Book 2)
https://www.amazon.com/dp/B08LP769LX
Family Ties (Book3)
https://www.amazon.com/gp/product/B08Q5GZHN3/
STANDALONES
Cabin Commotion
https://www.amazon.com/dp/B079Y29G5V/

Playboy Blaze is the son of Sal Bossio, a New York City Italian mobster. His father orders him to his Vermont cabin for one month while he settles mob business. Blaze hires a rent boy for one month, but unexpected events occur, and he finds himself alone in Vermont. When he reaches his cabin, he finds a stranger sleeping in his bed. The gorgeous gingered-haired man could be a hitman sent by his father's enemies.

High-paid escort Marcus graduates college and he's ready to leave The Manor. Working for pimp Kalepo for four years, Marcus believes there's no way out without paying a fatal price. Marcus leaves California on a train to New York City and a bus to a rented Vermont cabin for one month to hide from Kalepo.

Two lonely men solve the cabin commotion by sharing the only bed in the cabin during their sex fest saving hidden pasts and tough decisions until the month ends.

Sir Ethan's Contract
https://www.amazon.com/dp/B07DZ18WZ7

Rich, intelligent, and ridiculously sexy, Sir Ethan finds his submissive left him, breaking their D/s contract. Not wanting to be alone, Sir Ethan places an ad, offering a large sum of money for a submissive man. He wants to take care of a submissive, make rules, and dish out the consequences.

American born Adrien Dubois loses his family when ICE deports them to France. He hooks up with a mean ex-felon in a dilapidated campervan. When Stone abandons him, Adrien finds an ad for a submissive.

Sir Ethan is going to be Adrien's Dominant for one month, and he'll make lots of money. What could go wrong? He's going to take care of Adrien, and all he has to do is follow Sir Ethan's rules or his Dominant will spank him. Adrien is terrified to admit it, deep down he knows that soon he'll beg Sir Ethan to strip him bare and teach Adrien what happens to bad boys.

Two men dumped not looking for love, one needs money, and the other wants convenient sex.

Leather Paddles

https://www.amazon.com/Leather-Paddles-Brina-Brady-ebook/dp/B082FVS7LP/

He's had it with Doms. Never again...but maybe this one is different.

Twenty-two-year-old Jesse finds himself abandoned by his abusive Dom after four years in an unhappy BDSM relationship. Devastated, he moves in with his best friend, Charlie, and his Dom. He attends college and works in the university library. He doesn't have time nor plans to look for another Dom.

Master Andrew, the owner of BDSM club Leather Paddles, lost his husband five years ago. Ever since, he plays with different subs and is perfectly happy to leave it with that. He doesn't want another boy to call his own.

Once Master Andrew meets Jesse, things click for both of them, but Jesse remains skittish about getting involved with anyone. However, Master Andrew comes up with a plan to rein Jesse in his playroom and his heart.

Other people keep interfering, trying to separate the couple. Are Master Andrew and Jesse up to the challenge to move forward to their happily ever after?

Leather Paddles is a stand-alone MM romance featuring an insecure boy and a strict but caring Master. It has BDSM elements and a guaranteed HEA.

Baby Bear

https://www.amazon.com/dp/B0893L5694/

Abel's heartbreaking childhood contributes to his emotional baggage; his life has been one of hate, denial, and secrecy. His father, a polygamist cult leader, sends young men away from the compound in Utah so at eighteen, his mother drives him to the city. A dancing job opportunity finds Abel moving to Minnesota. Two years later he's mysteriously fired. Without savings, Abel needs a Daddy to take care of him, and he's found the perfect one at the Blue Diamond Diner.

Diner owner Darius Eriksen's dream is to find a boy who needs a Papa Bear to take care of his needs. Darius belongs to the Bearded Papa Bears. Membership requires Papa Bears wanting to be a daddy to a boy; they pledge to love, care, and discipline their Baby Bear. Two years after Darius's Baby Bear leaves him for another Papa Bear, he's ready to find a new Baby Bear and commit again.

Irish Traveller

Irish Traveller/Romani/gay boyfriends/Tarot Cards/Missing red-haired girls/

US Link: https://www.amazon.com/dp/B0931928VK

The disturbing disappearance of yet another young, red-haired gal from the Irish Travellers' Caravan has everyone on edge. Then Shamus Maguire's twelve-year-old sister Erin vanishes.

While searching for clues to his sister's disappearance, Shamus meets Lash Boswell, an older man from a Romani caravan. Lash decides to help Shamus, and they set out together to find the truth about the many disappearances.

Both their families disapprove of openly gay relationships. However, the tarot cards say these two are fated to be together. But to go public with their relationship, both would have family and friends forced to choose who they'll stay true to, the family or Lash and Shamus.

Can a Romani and an Irish Traveller make their relationship work without alienating their families? More importantly can they work together to find Erin?

All the Dark Lies

US: https://www.amazon.com/dp/B0992ZPL27

International link: mybook.to/AlltheDarkLies

Nathan leaves behind his life in a small town in Pennsylvania to move to London for a man he's never seen. After months of chatting online with the mysterious Charles promising the world, Nathan agrees to be the man's sub with the hope his life will change. One big problem, Nathan is a virgin and has only had virtual relationships.

When Nathan arrives in London, Charles is nowhere in sight, only a limo driver with mysterious instructions. He drives Nathan to a hotel where he stays overnight, then delivers him to the address of Lawrence, the handsome man, who he sat next to on the plane to London.

Both of them have told so many lies and half-truths. When all the dark lies threaten to come between them, is it too late for Charles and Nathan to come clean with each other?

Age Gap. Headmaster Dom, Virgin Sub, Lies and Secrets, Light BDSM, and HEA

House Arrest Without a Home
https://www.amazon.com/dp/B09NCFS67K
Shawn O'Brien

Pre-law student Shawn O'Brien loses his mind when he finds his live-in boyfriend Jasper Logan with a younger man in their bed. Shawn breaks the law and ends up in big trouble, in danger of losing his scholarship and freedom. He needs a new place to live to serve his house arrest sentence or he will go to jail for six months.

Noah Braun

Successful, District Prosecuting Attorney, Noah Braun has it all: money, friends, and a top career, but he's at risk of losing it all as he grieves the loss of his husband. His father, Judge Braun finds the perfect lover to save his son. The judge asks Noah to take Shawn into his home to complete his sentence.

Everything changes when Noah and Shawn meet and find themselves living together. Noah is determined to do whatever it takes to prove to Shawn that their relationship will be different from his nightmarish one with Jasper.

Can Noah find a way to win Shawn's heart forever, or will Shawn move on when his house arrest is complete?

Steamy, Age Gap, Hurt and Comfort, Contemporary, Forced Proximity, Destined to Be Together

Redeeming Jayden
https://www.amazon.com/dp/B09Z9R2H5B
JAYDEN BARRON

Twenty-two-year-old artist Jayden Barron is summoned home from New York City by his father to assist in the family business of painting and selling replica art to international rogue buyers. Nothing prepares him for what he encounters when he arrives, however, his entire family is missing.

Those his father has been dealing with rarely return missing people alive. The family attorney sends Jayden out of the country for his protection, straight into a haunted castle with a singing ghost who leaves him lilacs in the middle of the night. Fortunately, the castle also has Harlan Wendell.

HARLAN WENDELL

Affluent, generous, thirty-two-year-old, German interpreter, Harlan Wendell has every material possession he could want, but no love in his life. He hires young Jayden to recreate his family portraits lost in a fire. It isn't long before he realizes that Jayden is much more than an employee to him, and they begin a relationship that fulfills both their desires.

When events take a dramatic turn and secrets are revealed, can Harlan protect Jayden and their love?

Age Gap, Rogue Artist, German Translator, Haunted Castle, Missing Family, Secrets, Steamy, MM Romance Suspense, HEA, KU

Box Sets

Mobsters' Gay Sons Series Box Set

https://www.amazon.com/gp/product/B09RMSMKT4/

Irish Runaway Series Box Set

https://www.amazon.com/Irish-Runaway-Box-Set-Books1-3-ebook/dp/B09RW8V3C6/

Buried Secrets Series Box Set

https://www.amazon.com/Buried-Secrets-Box-Set-Books-ebook/dp/B09S4M35ZD/

Troubled Boys Bundle Box Set

https://www.amazon.com/dp/B0B5M4G6SN

All my audiobooks are on Audible here:

https://www.audible.com/author/Brina-Brady/B00KMW8LD4